Who is Scotland's Prettiest Princess?

Written by R_____
Illustrated by Annabel Spenceley

CHILDHOOD DREAMS
HOMETOWN WORLD

Everyone in the palace is very excited.
The handsome prince is hosting
a Grand Ball. He has written
lots of golden invitations.

Dear ....

Everyone keeps telling me to marry a princess. But I don't want to marry a princess! I want to marry my one true love. I will think she is the prettiest and loveliest girl in Scotland. I'm holding a Grand Ball at Inverness Castle so that I can meet her and dance with her.

I hope you can come!

The Prince

There is just one question on everyone's lips...

Who is the prince going to choose?

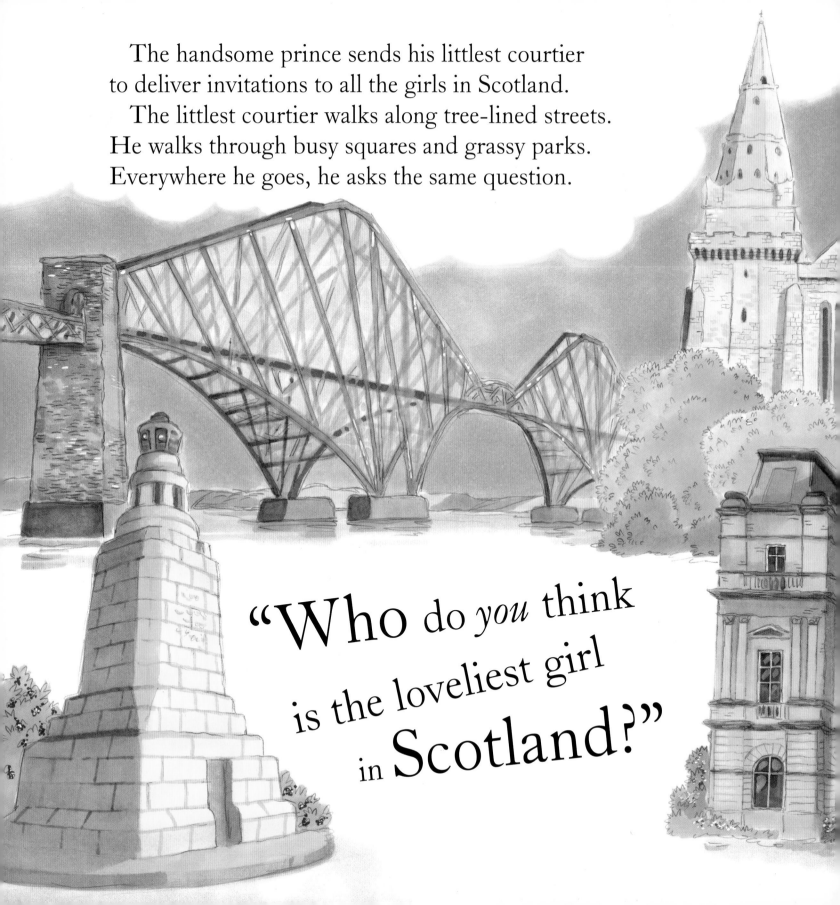

The handsome prince sends his littlest courtier
to deliver invitations to all the girls in Scotland.
    The littlest courtier walks along tree-lined streets.
He walks through busy squares and grassy parks.
Everywhere he goes, he asks the same question.

"Who do *you* think is the loveliest girl in Scotland?"

The littlest courtier asks
some children visiting the
People's Palace in Glasgow.
"Holly has the
sweetest smile,"
says a little girl.

Holly is full of **fun**.
She lives in a castle in
Aberdeen.

She has tumbling
golden curls and big
blue eyes, and she loves
dressing up best of all.

When the littlest courtier
gives her the golden invitation,
she smiles sweetly
and does

cartwheels

all around the castle!

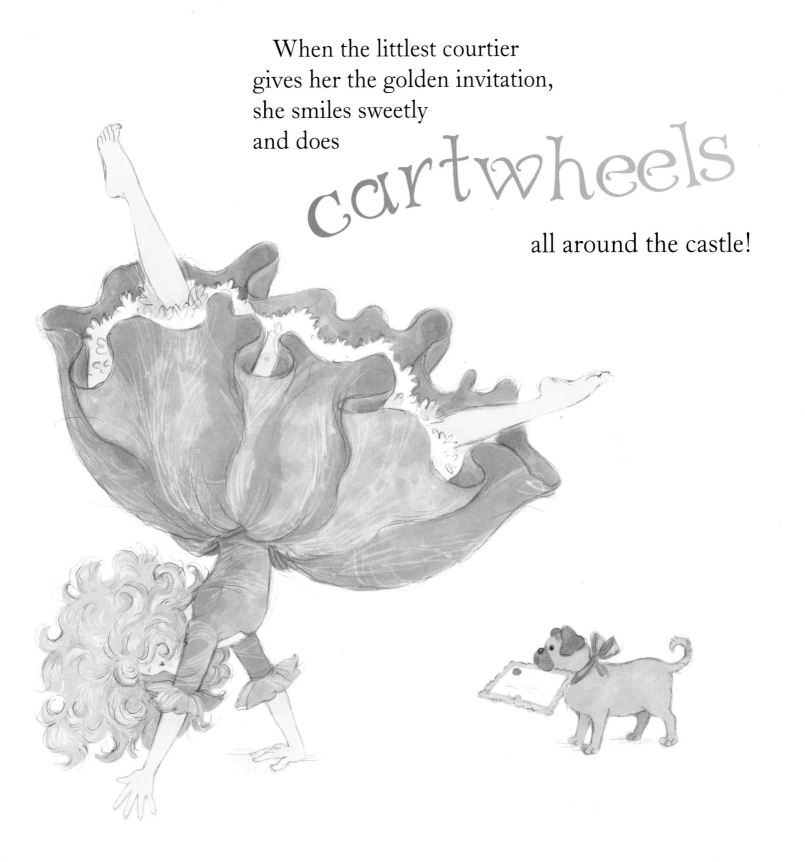

Holly is very excited to be invited to the ball. She goes to Union Street in Aberdeen to buy a new dress.

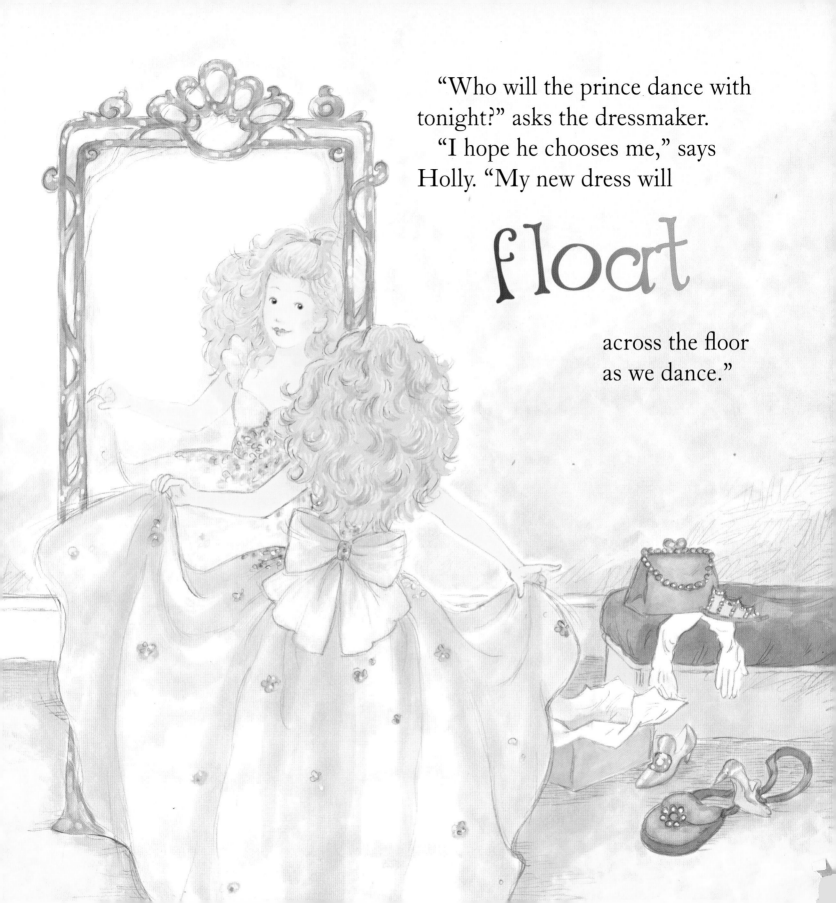

"Who will the prince dance with tonight?" asks the dressmaker.
"I hope he chooses me," says Holly. "My new dress will

float

across the floor as we dance."

The littlest courtier meets an old gardener in South Inch Park in Perth.

"Who do you think is the loveliest girl in Scotland?" he asks.

"Rani has the kindest eyes," says the old gardener.

Rani is very graceful. She lives in a grand house in Perth. She has thick brown ringlets and sparkling hazel eyes, and she loves dancing best of all.

Ding dong!

The littlest courtier rings the clanging doorbell and gives Rani the invitation. Her eyes twinkle kindly.

Rani can't wait for the ball to start! She goes to Edinburgh to buy a new pair of dancing shoes.

"**Who** will the prince dance with tonight?"

asks the shoemaker.

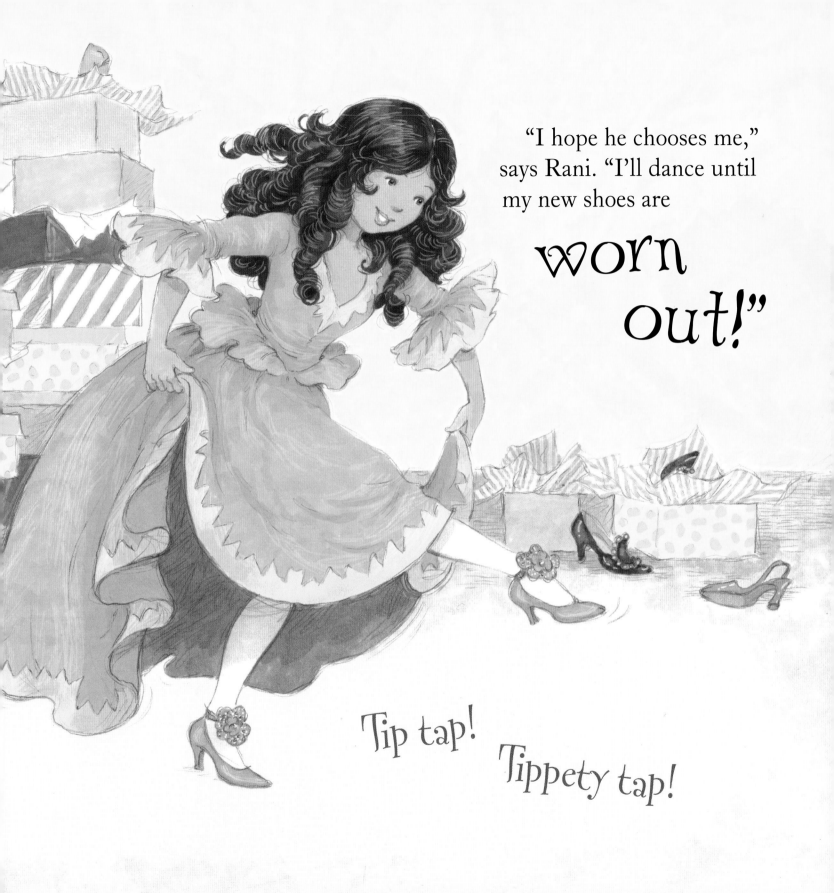

"I hope he chooses me," says Rani. "I'll dance until my new shoes are

worn out!"

Tip tap!

Tippety tap!

The littlest courtier meets a clown doing magic tricks in Dundee.

"Who do you think is the loveliest girl in Scotland?" he asks.

"Sophia has the cutest giggle," says the clown.

Sophia is very gentle. She lives in a house at the top of Dundee Law, and she loves **sequins** best of all.

She has a **shiny** black bob and **glimmering brown** eyes.

Sophia giggles in excitement as the littlest courtier gives her the golden invitation.

Sophia goes to Stirling and buys a sequinned headband.

It sparkles gold and silver.

"Who will the prince dance with tonight?"
asks the jeweller.

"I hope he chooses me," says Sophia. "My headband will glitter under the

chandeliers!"

The courtier meets a chimney sweep in Paisley.

"Who do you think is the loveliest girl in Scotland?" he asks.

"Chloe has the most enchanting voice," says the chimney sweep.

Chloe lives in a pretty cottage in Kilmarnock, and she loves MUSIC best of all.

She has big bouncy curls and deep brown eyes. When the littlest courtier gives Chloe her invitation, she sings happily.

The littlest courtier runs around Scotland all day long. From Falkirk to Fife, from Dumfries to Dunfermline, from Kirkcaldy to St Andrews and everywhere in between, he makes sure that every girl is invited.

The littlest courtier
delivers his last
invitation just as
the sun is beginning
to set. Feeling tired
but content, he turns
and walks back to
the palace.

The sun sets and the moon and stars start to glimmer.

Lots of girls arrive outside Inverness Castle.

The street is filled with the sound of laughter.

Dresses are rustling.

Sequins are sparkling.

It's time for the ball to start!

Inside the castle there is a spotless shiny dance floor.

The band is playing
beautiful
music.

The chandeliers are
shimmering
in the candlelight.

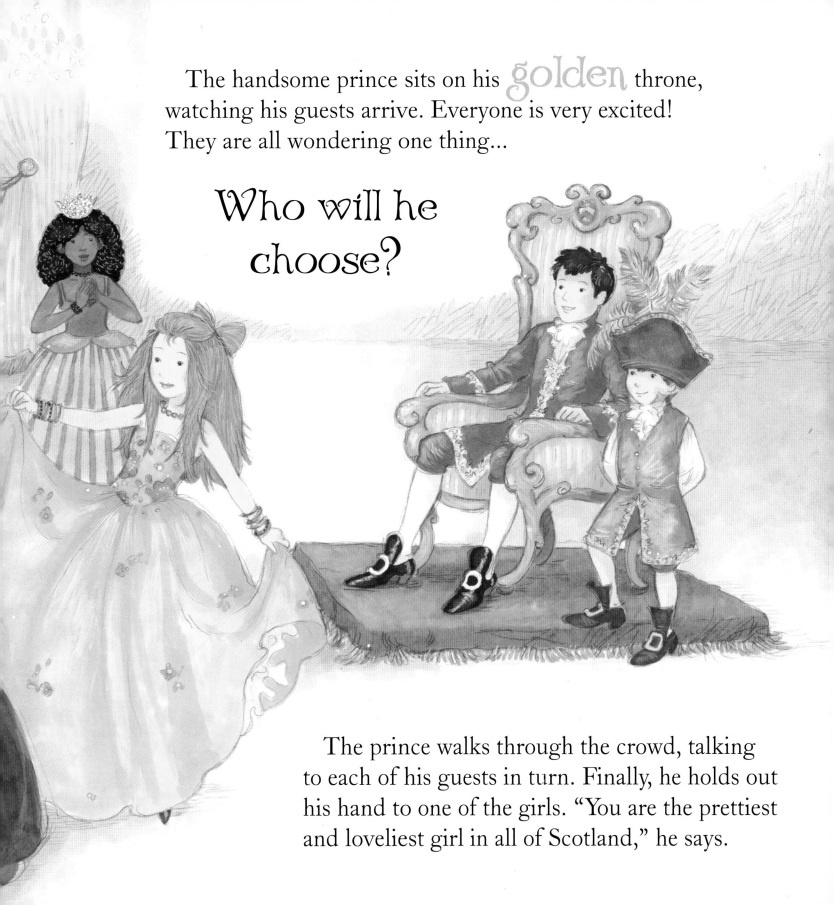

The handsome prince sits on his golden throne, watching his guests arrive. Everyone is very excited! They are all wondering one thing...

Who will he choose?

The prince walks through the crowd, talking to each of his guests in turn. Finally, he holds out his hand to one of the girls. "You are the prettiest and loveliest girl in all of Scotland," he says.

The handsome prince dances with his one true love. He will marry her and make her **a princess!**

But **WHO IS** his chosen princess?

It's YOU!